There is a loud rumbling noise on the farm. Baa is scared and he runs away!

Read aloud   Read along

Baa dived into Jess' basket.

"I wouldn't be so scared if I knew what the noise was!" said Baa, hiding under the blankets.

Then Jess had a thought.

"Hey! That's it, Baa! That's the big question. What's the grumbly, rumbly noise?"

Jess and Baa set off to find the answer.

Jess has a big question!
What's the grumbly, rumbly noise?

First stop was the Lily Pond. The noise sounded a bit like a drum. Maybe it was Horace playing with his instruments?

"How about this for a rumble?" smiled Horace.

Horace picked up his sticks and banged on his hollow log drum.

Bang! Bang! Bang!

It was very loud, but it wasn't the grumbly, rumbly noise.

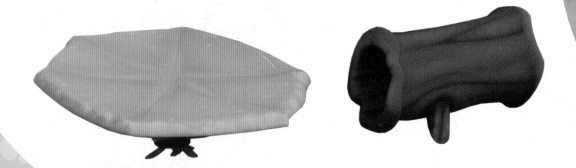

Maybe the rumbly noise is Horace's drum?
No, the drum only makes a BANG!

Read aloud   Read along

The loud rumble crashed around the farm again.

"Hey, it sounds like it's coming from up high," said Horace.

"Hmm, clouds are made from raindrops," said Jess, looking up at the sky. "But water doesn't growl!"

If the noise wasn't Horace's drum or the clouds, then what could it be?

The rumble noise crashes around the farm. Horace thinks it is coming from the sky.

Read aloud   Read along

Baa didn't want to hang around to
find the answer. He hid behind a bush.

"Come on, Baa," said Jess. "You don't need
to be scared, I promise.
Let's go and see if we
can find some more clues."

Baa poked his head around the bush.

"Ooh, I do want to help you find the answer,"
Baa trembled. "But I don't like that noise!"

Read alone

Baa hides behind a bush.
He is too scared to find the answer.

Read aloud   Read along

Just then, a bright light flashed across the sky!

"Woah!" said Horace. "That's so cool!"

"Wow! What was that?" Jess gasped. "Now we've got to find out what the grumbly noise is and what the big light is."

Read alone

A bright light flashes across the sky!
What can it be?

When the flash of light had gone, the grumbly noise rumbled in the sky again. Baa ran back to the barn. He wasn't sticking around for any more noises or flashing lights!

Horace chuckled. "Well, I think it's amazing. I'm going chill in my pond and watch the light show. Good luck with finding your answers, Jess!"

Read alone

Baa runs back to the barn, but Horace stays to watch the flashing lights.

Read aloud   Read along

Over at the barn, Jinx and Joey had seen the bright lights, too. They were very excited when Jess arrived.

"Maybe the flashing light is a big spaceship!" giggled Joey.

"Or a firework!" said Jinx.

Jess laughed. "I don't think it's a spaceship or a firework, but I do think it has something to do with the sky. If only we had another clue!"

Read alone

Jinx and Joey watch the bright lights, too.
Joey thinks it's a spaceship!

Read aloud   Read along

Meanwhile, Billie was following a clue of her own. She had found a brown paper bag with apples in.

She carefully emptied out the apples and blew up the bag.

When Jess wasn't looking, Billie jumped on top of the blown-up bag and ... POP!

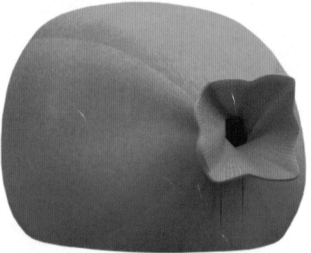

Read alone

Billie tries to make a rumbling noise.
She blows up a paper bag. POP!

Baa jumped up into the air again!

"Sorry, Baa!" giggled Billie. "I thought I could make the sound of the rumbly noise."

"Great idea, Billie. But it didn't make a loud enough noise," said Jess. "I know someone who has lots and lots of paper. She might be making the noise! Can you guess who it is?"

"Mimi!" shouted out Baa and Billie.

Billie's popping noise isn't the rumbling sound. But maybe Mimi can help.

Jess and the gang raced over to Mimi's hutch. They quickly told her all about the grumbly noise and the popping bag.

"So now we need something really big to burst," said Jess. "Then we can see if it makes the rumbling sound!"

Mimi searched through her art box and pulled out a red balloon.

"This might do it!" said Mimi.

Mimi finds a balloon. If she pops it, will it make the rumbly noise?

Read aloud   Read along

Mimi pumped up the balloon.
Soon it was bigger than Jess!

"Woah!" said Jess. "That's the biggest
balloon I've ever seen."

"You burst it, Jess," said Billie. "Let's see
if it makes the grumbly, rumbly noise!"

The friends were very excited to find out!
On the count of three, Jess got ready to jump
on top of the giant balloon.

1, 2, 3 ...

Mimi pumps up the balloon.
Soon it is bigger than Jess!

Read aloud   Read along

BANG!

The bursting balloon made a very loud sound, but it wasn't the noise in the sky.

"Hmm ... if it's not Horace's drum, or the clouds, or a popping bag, or a bursting balloon, then what is the grumbly, rumbly noise?" asked Jess, puzzled.

Read alone

Jess bursts the balloon. BANG!
But it isn't the grumbly, rumbly noise.

Read aloud   Read along

Just then, Willow arrived. Jess told
her about the flashing lights in the sky.

"Oh, you mean lightning," said Willow.
"The flashes in the sky are called lightning."

Just then, some more lightning lit up the sky.
Seconds later, the grumbly noise echoed around
the farm again.

Jess had a thought. "The grumbly noise always
comes after the lightning. Maybe the noise has
something to do with the lightning ..."

Willow tells the gang the flashing lights in the sky are called lightning.

"That's very clever, Jess!" said Willow. "The grumbly noise is called thunder. Lightning is always followed by thunder ..."

"Thunder is the sound that lightning makes!" said Jess. "That's the grumbly noise! It's thunder! We've found the answer! Yippety yay!"

"Hurray!" The gang jumped up and down.

Just then, big sploshes of rain fell from the sky. The friends ran inside to watch the storm, and this time even Baa enjoyed the grumbly, rumbly noise!

The grumbly noise is the sound of the lightning! It is called thunder. Jess found the answer! Yippety yay! Hurray!

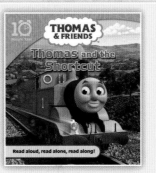

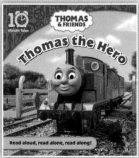

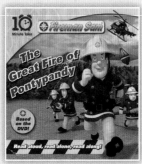

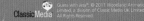